Moki the Gecko's

BEST CHRISTMAS EVER

by

Bruce Hale

WORDS + PICTURES

PUBLISHING, INC

Other Moki the Gecko books you may enjoy:
Legend of the Laughing Gecko
Surf Gecko to the Rescue!
The Adventures of Space Gecko
Moki and the Magic Surfboard

Mahalo plenty to the helpful hands and eyes of Brian Reed, Jim Rumford and Marie Miyashiro.

Library of Congress Catalog Card Number: 98-090235
ISBN: 0-9621280-6-6

Printed in Hong Kong.

This book is dedicated to my wife, Janette,
who makes every day
seem like Christmas.

Fast asleep under a hula moon, Moki the Gecko lay dreaming of a green Christmas. Shimmering waves crooned a holiday tune. Graceful palm trees danced a lazy Christmas Eve mambo.

Moki waited for Christmas morning.

But little did he know, out over the blue Pacific, something was wrong.

That same Christmas Eve, while Moki
dreamed, Santa Claus landed in a heap
of trouble. Halfway to Hawaii, a feather-
brained frigate bird spooked Santa's reindeer.
Dasher bumped Dancer
and Comet kicked Vixen.
And humbledy-jumble,
they tumbled from the sky —
antlers over hooves, Santa over sleigh —
into the ocean: Ka-sploosh!

Wet reindeer, soggy presents and a not-so-jolly St. Nick bobbed on the swells. Santa's reindeer were too wet for take-off. How would they ever get airborne?

"Sorry, big fella," Santa told Dasher. "Looks like no Christmas for the Island children."

"No Christmas? No way!" said a cheerful voice. Santa turned to see Kealii the Dolphin swimming by.

"Can you help us?" said Santa. "My reindeer must dry off before they can fly."

Kealii tried towing the team to a nearby island, but they were far too heavy.

"We need help," said the dolphin. "I'll get my friend, Moki the Gecko. He's the best surfer around, even with his beat-up old board."

As he left, Kealii said, "By the way, watch out for the Lone Shark. She lives around here and she doesn't like anybody — except as a snack."

"Great," said Santa. "We should have stayed at the North Pole. Polar bears I can handle."

Kealii raced to his friend's house.

"Moki!" he yelled. "Come help!"

Sleepy-eyed, the gecko peered out his window. "Is it Christmas, yet?" he yawned.

"If we don't hurry, there won't be any Christmas," said the dolphin. He explained Santa's trouble.

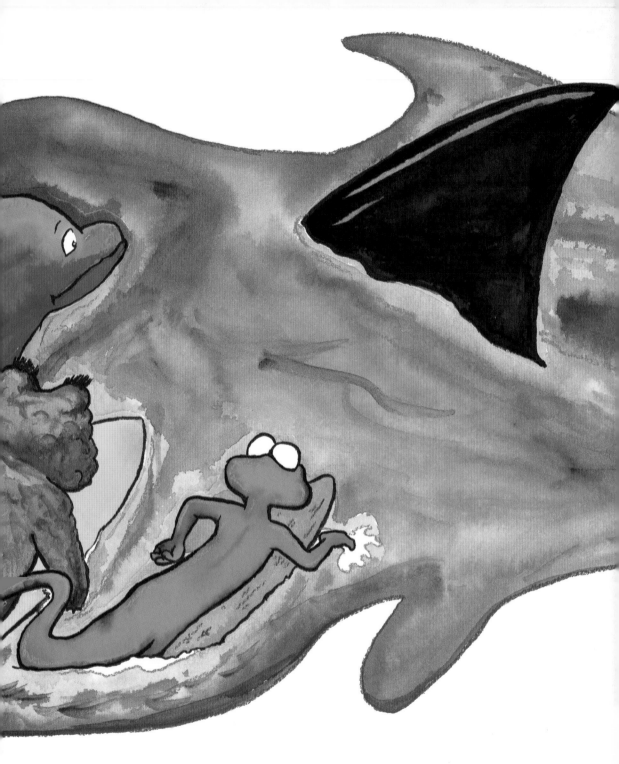

Moki jumped into action. He grabbed his old surfboard and some good friends. They paddled pell-mell for
Santa's sleigh. But just before they reached it, Moki and
his friends saw something that chilled their bones.
    A tall gray fin sliced the water. The Lone Shark!

The giant shark circled Santa and his reindeer. She flashed a jumbo mouthful of sharp teeth. "Yum, yum," she said. "Reindeer sushi! And for dessert, Santa Surprise."

Lone Shark snapped at the surfers, driving them back.

"Let's all rush her at once," said Kealii. "She can't get all of us." But nobody moved. Nobody wanted to face the jaws of death.

"Hurry!" said Kealii. "If we don't think fast, there'll never be another Christmas!" Lone Shark circled closer. She licked her sharky lips.

"I know!" said Moki to the shark. "We'll catch something for you. How about some yummy fish?"

"Fish, fish, fish!" shouted the Lone Shark. "I'm bored with fish. I eat fish for breakfast, lunch and dinner. I want some North Pole treats."

Comet and Cupid whimpered. Blitzen tried to hide behind some seaweed.

Moki's mind raced. How sad Christmas would be without Santa and his gifts. He grabbed a box off the sleigh and handed it to the Lone Shark.

"Here — how about a Christmas present?" Moki said. "You've lived alone for so long. I bet you've never had a present."

The Lone Shark glared. "A present?" she snapped. "I've got no friends and I've got no presents! Who needs them?"

She swatted the box into the water with a leathery flipper.

Moki sighed. Then his eyes lit up. He whispered to Kealii, who led the other surfers out of sight.

"Don't you ever get afraid?" Moki asked the shark. "Living out here alone in the dark?"

"Never," said the beast. "I'm the biggest and toughest. Who could scare me?"

"What about the Great Gaboolah?" said Moki. "Even mighty whales fear the Great Gaboolah."

"Nice try," said the Lone Shark. "Never heard of the Great Big Ghoulash."

Just then, Moki pointed. "Behind you!" he cried.
"It's... it's... the Great Gaboolah!"

The shark turned, and a huge shadowy creature
floated on the waves. It stretched toward the moon,
dripping seaweed.

"Swim for your life!" shouted Moki.

The shark froze. As she watched, the Great Gaboolah swayed left, then right, then fell — ker-flump! Seaweed and surfers tumbled into the sea.

Lone Shark smiled her sharky smile. "Trying to trick me, eh?" she said. "Too late — it's suppertime. Say 'aloha 'oe' to Christmas."

She swam toward the sleigh with jaws open wide.
"Wait! Doesn't Santa get a last wish?" asked Moki.
"Huh? Oh, all right," huffed the shark. "But hurry up.
I'm hungry."

Santa Claus sighed and gazed sadly at his reindeer. "Well, if this is my last Christmas," he said, "how about a last Christmas carol?"

Moki and his friends were so sad they could barely talk, but who could refuse Santa's last wish? Softly, raggedly, they started to sing.

The sweet melody swelled. The singers gained strength as it went on, and the old tune echoed over the dark water. The last note seemed to hang in the salty air forever.

In the silence that followed, Moki heard a faint sound. He turned and saw the shark sniffling and water-eyed.

"Merry Christmas, Lone Shark," he said.

"Oh, Merry Christmas," she muttered. "Now, where's that present?"

Moki fished the box from the water and handed it to her. The shark grabbed the gift and shredded its wrapping. Inside was the tiniest rubber ducky you ever saw.

Santa and his reindeer held their breath for a heart-beat or two. Then the Lone Shark smiled — her first real smile. "Merry Christmas, everyone!" she shouted. "And many more to come!"

Then Lone Shark took the twisted reins in her teeth and towed Santa's sleigh to the nearest island, faster than you could say, "ho ho ho."

Moki and his friends built a bonfire. The other animals untangled the sleigh, while the reindeer and Santa dried themselves by the dancing flames.

Finally, Santa and his team were ready. They took to the sky in a sprinkle of sand and stardust. Quick as a wink, Santa delivered presents all over the Islands.

A yawning Moki the Gecko headed home with his friends.

The next morning, Christmas morning, he jumped out of bed and ran to the gecko Christmas tree. There Moki found the usual presents, but near the door, he saw the biggest package of all.

Moki tore the wrapping off a new surfboard, autographed by all the reindeer and Santa, himself. It said:

To Moki the Gecko,
whose Christmas spirit shines so bright.
May all your rides be smooth and clean,
and may all your Christmases be green.